Glimpses of Gauguin

Glimpses of Gauguin

Maryann D'Agincourt

PP

Portmay Press

New York

The sketch on pages 31–34 first appeared in *Able Muse* as "Autumn Whorl."

Cover image: Paul Gauguin, French, 1848–1903, *Where Do We Come From? What Are We? Where Are We Going?*, 1897–98, Oil on canvas 139.1 x 374.6 cm (54¾ x 147½ in.), Museum of Fine Arts, Boston, Tompkins Collection—Arthur Gordon Tompkins Fund, 36.270.

Cover design by Emily Albarillo

Printed in the United States of America
First published in 2014 by Portmay Press, New York
This paperback edition published in 2019 by Portmay Press, New York
ISBN 978-0-9994006-7-8 (pb)

Publisher's Cataloging-in-Publication
(Provided by Quality Books, Inc.)
D'Agincourt, Maryann.
Glimpses of Gauguin / by Maryann D'Agincourt.
pages cm
ISBN 978-0-9891745-5-8 (hc)
ISBN 978-0-9891745-6-5 (ebook)
1. Art--Fiction. 2. Artists--Fiction. 3. Families--Fiction. 4. Interpersonal relations--Fiction. 5. Domestic fiction. I. Title.
PS3604.A332544G55 2014 813'.6
QBI14-1992

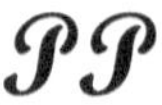

Portmay Press
244 Madison Avenue
New York, NY 10016
www.portmaypress.com

Also by Maryann D'Agincourt

Journal of Eva Morelli
All Most
Printz
Shade and Light

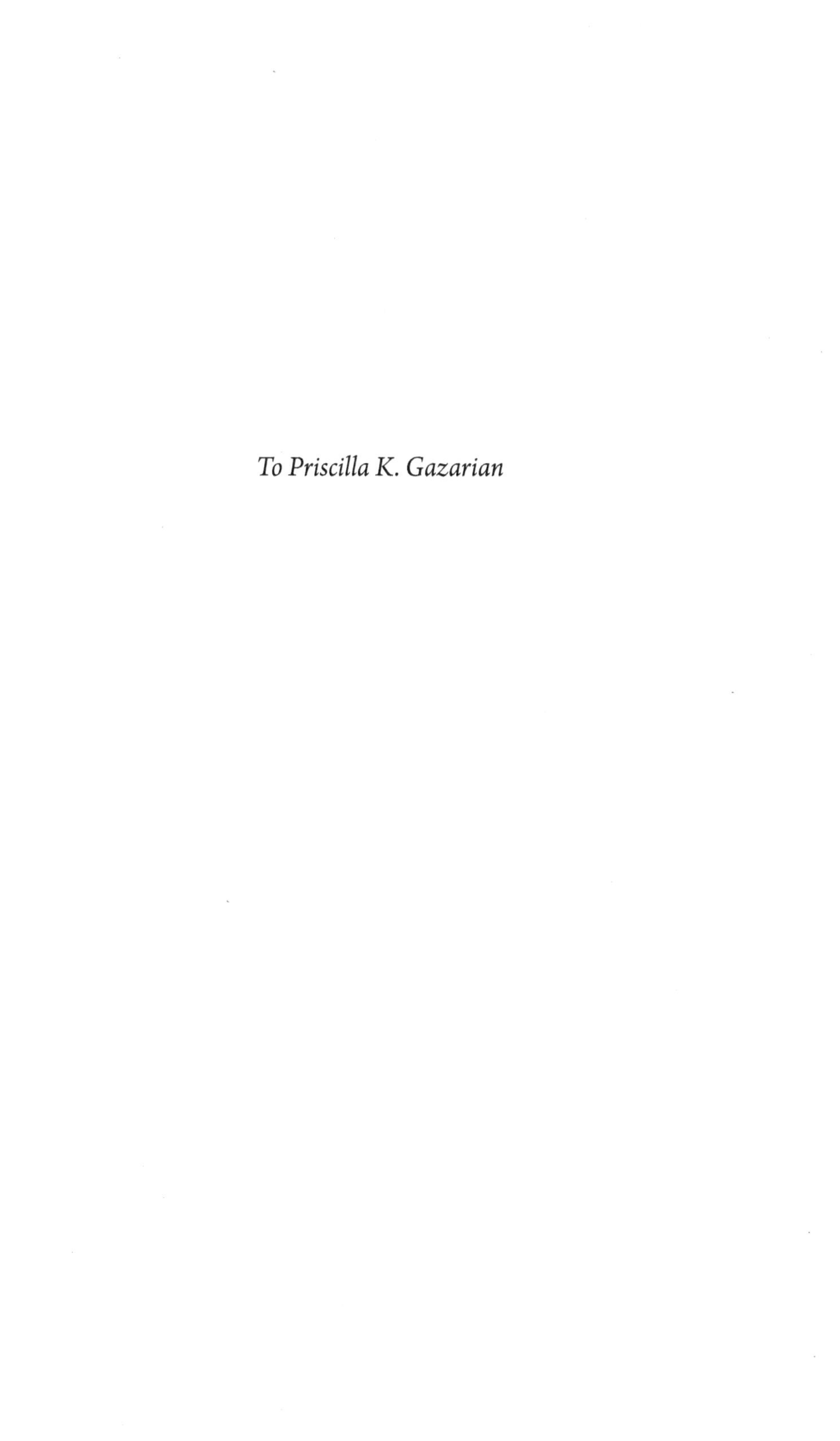

To Priscilla K. Gazarian

My deepest appreciation goes to Emily Albarillo, the editor of these pages—as always, her work reflects her intelligence, sensitivity to language, and keen insight.

Art requires philosophy, just as
philosophy requires art. Otherwise,
what would become of beauty?

—Paul Gauguin

D'où Venons-Nous
Where Do We Come From?

I recall the steady whirr of the ceiling fan and then blinds tapping the window frame. And how in my dream there was a cry.

Florida, summer 1962

I grope in the dark, rub my fist against the wall as if gripping a match, attempting to strike a flame. My feet brush the carpet; the heat is enclosing. I make my way down the hallway. Faintly I hear voices whispering into the night. I push open a door.

A soft light casts shadows across the room. Both my mother and father are sitting up, a sheet covering them, their heads pressing against satin pillows. A breeze lifts the silky white drapes. I linger in the doorway. My mother's round arms are pale and limp. Her scattered hair grazes her shoulders as she turns toward me. "Jocelyn," she calls out, leaning forward, clutching the sheet to her chest. Languidly she beckons for me to come in. I curl up at the foot of their bed, gazing at the floating silk drapes and open door.

My father's voice is deep and groggy. "Alex Martaine, he's a painter . . . a painter from Canada—Ottawa, I believe," he tells her, as if he's given much thought to what he's saying. "He's coming to teach at Pierson. Though his style is quite different, they say his use of color, his interpretation of it, may be like Gauguin's."

My mother whispers a response. I'm uncertain of her words, but the feeling and mood they create excite me.

I cannot sleep and remain on their bed, my chin propped up against the pillow she's handed me. Fixedly I stare past the doorway, my heart beating uncontrollably. For I believe at any moment Alex Martaine will come into the room and turn our lives around.

1967

"You identify a painting by the artist's stroke," she says, her voice subdued and edgy. "The soft brush of a Renoir, the clean lines of a Matisse, the round turns in a Gauguin." Her hair is gathered into a barrette, her hooded jacket loose and open. I listen closely as she guides me through the Museum of Fine Arts in Boston. It is a mid-April afternoon, the day my lessons begin.

My mother and I climb a long marble stairway and soon

find ourselves in a huge and shadowy room. Looming tapestries with vague and distant figures cover the walls. For a moment she stops, squinting up at one with a unicorn. Before I realize it, she's moving on.

With sketchbook in hand, I follow her swaying form across the parquet floor and through a long, wide hallway with gold-framed paintings on either side. Then she turns right, and we are in a high-ceilinged room. Not looking back, she says, "Let's start with Gauguin." The hem of her pink woolen skirt caresses her knees, a tear in her nylon stocking showing above her ankle. Again she stops, pointing out Gauguin's *Women and a White Horse.* She doesn't want me to copy the entire painting, just to imitate the artist's stroke as best I can.

As she leans over to look at my work, her hazel eyes flickering over my faint sketching, her cheek brushes the top of my head. Strands of her fine hair escape from the barrette. I am her first and only student.

A brisk April breeze comes through the half-open kitchen window; holding my pencil tightly, I carefully copy on a sheet of white lined paper a poem, "The Tyger," by William Blake.

I feel a firm tap on my shoulder. When I look up, she's standing close, holding up a magazine; on the cover is a sketch of a woman's face worked in swirling lines. "Jocelyn, this is a Martaine," she exclaims, handing it to me.

I bring the magazine up to my eyes, pretend to study the cover, feel my face growing red. "I hate it!" I cry out, hearing panic in my voice, and slap the magazine facedown on the table. As I run upstairs to my bedroom, my eyes fill with tears.

My mother calls out from the foot of the stairway, tapping her long nails against the banister. I imagine her chin slightly raised, her eyes veiled with concern as she anxiously asks, "Jocelyn, please tell me—what it is you don't like about Alex's sketch?"

One July morning, wrapped in the slowness of summer, I stand behind the screen door, my fingers touching the netting; I peer out at my mother in the backyard. Hose in hand, she waters the recently planted hydrangeas, looking off into the distance, the freshly mowed grass cushioning her bare feet. From time to time she sprays the wicker chair and table close to the flower bed.

As I've sensed her growing more restive each day, I watch her assiduously. Her shirt is unbuttoned at the top, revealing the top fringe of her white bra. Her auburn hair is tousled. When she's done watering, she drops the hose and thrusts back her shoulders, tilting her face toward the sky. With her hands on her fragile hips, her fingers hidden by the folds of her madras skirt, she squints, parting her lips as if in her unsettled way she's talking to the sun.

So immersed in her thoughts, I do not believe she hears the screen door open. Stealthily I come up behind her and throw my arms around her waist.

"I've had another bad dream," I whisper, burrowing my face in her taut back.

Her body tenses. Pulling my arms away, she turns around, her hands firm on my shoulders. Her cheeks are flushed from the strong sun and her eyes probe mine as if I'm speaking a foreign tongue. I know it bothers her that I—so much more intense, she's said, than she was at eleven—am having bad dreams already. Emotion touches her face, an innocuous, hesitant wave brushing the shore then receding; her features fall back into line.

In a measured way, I tell her about my dream. It's always the same. At the beginning of the dream I'm able to see and by the end of it, I am blind.

"You must be calm and steady, Jocelyn," she says, her voice firm, her smile wavering. What she does not realize is this dream allows me to communicate with her in a way I never would have if I'd not experienced it.

Squinting up at the sun again, her lower lip shaky, she says quietly, "We'll go to see Gracie." Visiting Gracie—will it erase my dream?

A gentle wind blows through the old and worn Mercedes that once belonged to my father's father. My mother drives along the curving coastline toward Gracie's apartment. There's not much traffic. She's refused to turn on the air conditioning. In the back seat, the hot upholstery stings my bare shoulders. As I gaze out the window at the swirling ocean I fan myself with a softcover copy of *The Arabian Nights*.

Soon we drive into the curved, paved entranceway of the familiar brick and ivy building, parking in the first space on the left.

The foyer is dark, the ceiling high; the rusting wrought-iron table against the wall appears unmovable. The heat is oppressive. Our footsteps echo as we walk to the elevator. She awkwardly opens the accordion-like door, and once we are inside, she presses a button and we are carried up to the third floor.

Gracie's apartment is number thirty-five. As my mother knocks below the gold numbers, her expression is focused. She presses her ear against the door, her lips parting. I tug at her pocketbook as if to stop her, my sense of anticipation growing.

Gracie opens the door a crack, peering at our flushed faces, her pale blue eyes searching. Then, closing the door, she unfastens the latch and lets us in. She reaches out and gathers us both in her long, sturdy arms. As she catches my gaze, she says, as she always does, her voice husky, "Jocelyn, you are small for your age. You'll not be as tall as your mother. Don't frown. You will be a petite woman—it will have its advantages."

Releasing us, she fluffs her red-gold hair and purses her fleshy lips. Her skin is flushed, her cheekbones high. On her thick red fingers she wears three rings set with large stones. I sniff the sweet hand cream she's lavishly applied. Abruptly she motions for us to sit on the stiff, antique sofa next to the window and then she disappears behind a Chinese screen in the far corner of the room.

Cascading sunlight illuminates every detail of Gracie's studio. The two windows are fully open. A dusty ray streams into the room past the parted lace curtains, caressing my mother's earnest profile. As she crosses her arms, her body relaxes into the hard sofa.

I imagine Gracie behind the black lacquered screen, stooping over a large box filled with jewelry. Angling my ear away from the open windows, away from the sound of the ocean, I hear her forceful rummaging.

Soon Gracie's thick hand wrestles the screen to the side. As she comes toward us, her blue dressing gown swishes and her eyes shine; entwined in her fingers is a strand of pearls.

Carefully, she holds out the necklace so that my mother and I can study it. Then she speaks: "I bought these in Majorca; they are old, very old, and may have belonged to a countess who escaped to Majorca during the French Revolution. Touch them, Lillian, Jocelyn, touch them, feel how smooth they are."

She grasps the necklace, her cheeks flushed.

"Try it on," Gracie insists.

"No, I don't need to—I'll buy the pearls," my mother says reflexively.

"Without trying them on? You must try things, Lillian, to see if they are right for you."

She adroitly clasps the pearls around my mother's neck, then points to the mirror above the small table.

With a sturdy elegance Gracie accompanies us down the dark, musty corridor to the elevator. "How is Alex?" my mother asks over her shoulder as she opens the door.

"Alex is self-absorbed, committed to his work, no different from any other painter. He's elusive. I'm tiring of him," Gracie responds emphatically.

As we step into the elevator, my mother says protectively, "I've heard he is quite talented."

"There are many talented people in the world, Lillian," Gracie boldly answers, the door closing her from our sight.

We walk through the dark foyer and out into the day; the sunlight is sharp and glaring

"Gracie was contrary today," she says pensively, breaking the silence in the car, the ocean to her left. The tide has come in.

I move forward to the edge of the seat, tap my mother's moist arm; half asking, half demanding, I tell her, "I want to hold the pearls."

With one hand on the steering wheel and the other groping inside her pocketbook, she soon pulls them out. "Be careful," she says, handing them to me, her eyes misty from the heat.

Noon. All the shades in the kitchen are drawn to block the heat. My mother's light, quick steps cross the room. She removes a pitcher of lemonade from the refrigerator.

From my seat at the kitchen table, I watch her. As she hands me a glass of cold lemonade, I ask her about the French Revolution.

She crosses her arms and leans against the counter. Sighing, she says, "There was no equality in France at that time, hundreds of years ago; things had to change. The French people were dissatisfied with their lives."

"Why did the countess escape to Majorca?" I ask.

"I don't know if that's accurate. I believe a countess would have worn genuine pearls—those are cultured," she says pointing to the long strand around my neck. Then she comes close and examines the pearls, lightly touching them.

"Does Gracie lie?" I ask, my voice high. I am shaken but not surprised.

"No," she says, stepping away, her wavering eyes defiant. "Gracie enhances the truth."

In my parents' bedroom, I lift the necklace over my head, place it on the bureau— against the shiny mahogany surface, the pearls look unappealing.

Outside, sitting on the front top step, I press my bare feet against the rough surface of the brick, my arms around my legs. It's very quiet and still, the hottest part of the day.

The screen door opens, startling me. I turn around and see my father. He comes and sits next to me. "Don't waste this summer day, Jocelyn," he says. There's a longing in his voice, his raised light red brows, his slumping shoulders.

And I think of the night not so long ago he came into my bedroom. He grasped the book I was reading and in its place put in my hands a collection of short stories by Chekhov. I held the hardbound book, watching shadows cross the cover. Soon he took it from me and began to read a story. It was called "The Huntsman." Leaning forward to catch the light from the small lamp next to my bed, he read in a dispassionate voice, his face flushed. I couldn't comprehend the meaning of the story; instead I pictured the hunting dog, the straight road, the silent forest, the hopeful expression on the face of the woman.

Today, I suppose, he'll meet his friends at the coffee shop on Crescent Street where the waitresses wear blue-checked aprons over gray uniforms and the linoleum floor is not well swept. Father and his acquaintances—policemen, firemen, some other teachers, the mayor—will meet and speak about their work, politics, the war in Vietnam, so very far away, people's lives, and then, lastly and quietly, their own personal secrets, hovering close to them like frightened children. As I sat next to him in the car on our way to the coffee shop last summer, he said, his voice reaching, that it was a place where everyone becomes equal.

Now I watch as he drives off, his elbow out the window. The heat intensifies and I go inside, heading straight for my bedroom. I fall onto the bed. The sheets are surprisingly cool.

The house feels empty. Shadows cross the bedroom floor. It's still light outdoors, early evening. I hear low voices coming from the living room. It's my mother and someone else.

There's something in the tone of her voice, something I've never heard before—a sharp, teasing note that makes me feel distant from her, that warns me not to intrude on her and her visitor, that if I do I'll be reprimanded. I open the bedroom door slightly and peer out past the stairway railing, down into the living room. Outside the large picture window I see the sun, a huge tangerine ball pinned to the sky. She sidles up to the window, pointing to the sun. She turns and looks across the room, her expression decided, her head slightly lowered.

It's as if I'm at the theater, watching a movie on a big screen, and my mother has now come in view of the camera. Again she turns to look at the sun, her hands on her hips, the way she stood this morning in the backyard.

I kneel, still peering through the long, narrow opening in the door. My mother has changed into her crimson skirt, a white off-the-shoulder blouse, and large gold-looped earrings.

She turns away from the window, gazing across the room. Her hands are clasped as if she's praying. When she smiles, her lips appear full and red.

"Happy birthday," she says. "Thank you for telling me. Most people wouldn't say it, you know." Her words flow into the summer evening. She tosses back her head, her neck long and yielding. She opens her hands, her fingers shaky.

Slowly he goes to her. He has straight dark hair and is much taller than she is. He bends his head, stands close to her. Her head is back, as if she's basking in the sun.

He grasps her bare shoulders, kissing her for a long, long time.

I squeeze my eyes shut and hear odd noises coming from their mouths, like the distant sound of crying birds.

When they separate they do not speak. As they walk toward the front door, I see his face—it's my father's friend, Mr. Martaine, the art teacher.

I hear the screen door open. "Lilly," he says, his voice forlorn.

"Sorry you missed Martin. You know how much I care for him," she answers uncertainly.

Him, my father, his presence suddenly evoked. All I've heard him say about Mr. Martaine is that he admires him because he went to Korea and because he's a painter—the pursuit of art requires much desire and commitment.

Once he leaves, I slip past my door and go up the hallway to my parents' bedroom.

The pearls are no longer on top of the bureau. I rummage through the bottom drawer where my mother keeps her jewelry. I toss aside nylon stockings until I find the pearls. Grasping the necklace with both hands, I raise it to my nose and sniff. The pearls are sweet and musty, like Gracie's hand cream, like Gracie's apartment.

I grip the necklace in one hand and with the other I hoist myself on top of my parents' unmade bed. As I study my reflection in the mirror above the bureau, I place the pearls over my head and drape them close to my neck so that the strand hangs long, loose down my back, like a train. I untie my halter top, feel it fall to my waist, and then pull the necklace forward and down, the pearls now thumping my bare chest. With the palm of my hand I press the necklace against my throat, the pearls hard and smooth. A sweet and achy sensation enfolds me as I close my eyes and kiss the air.

In the afternoon sun, fallen leaves still moist from a soft morning rainfall are strewn across the sidewalk like embers. On this breezy October day, I press my school folder to my chest to protect the papers inside from the wind. As I make my way home, I'm apprehensive, uncertain if my mother will be there. For I know my father won't be—he's now in New York during the week. He's received a fellowship and is writing a novel. In his absence, it's as if our home suddenly has a large hole in the center and my mother and I have to walk gingerly around its periphery. We're surprised to realize how much of a part he's played in holding the three of us together. So we occupy ourselves with other things, things that lead us away from the imagined dark hole.

One late September day, her eyes gleaming in the morning light, my mother told me that she'd enrolled in a course at the art museum, a seminar on Rembrandt, a graduate course.

I often find her in the middle of the night in the small study at the back of the house wrapped in her green velvet bathrobe, hunched over the typewriter, punching the keys. She's sleepy but determined; a half-filled cup of tea stands on the desk next to a small ebony lamp with a singed shade. Behind her chair I stand, watching. She doesn't turn her head to look at me. After a while she lifts her chin just a bit and stops typing, not turning around. Clacking a red-painted fingernail against one key, she says, "Jocelyn, it's time now to go to bed."

Fearful of disturbing her, my heart beating quickly, I tiptoe out of the room. She doesn't resume her work until I'm halfway down the hall.

She throws her whole self into writing papers about art. When she holds a page she's been working on in her hand, it's as if it's part of her body, another limb.

Slowly I begin to see a change in her; she's less critical than when my father's at home and less questioning of my whereabouts, but at the same time she's more affectionate toward me, more so than she's been in the past.

I reach home and ring the bell. When no one answers, I

use the key she's given me to let myself in. I go directly to the small study at the back of the house do to my homework. On the wall hangs a framed print of Gauguin's masterpiece, *Where Do We Come From? What Are We? Where Are We Going?* When I glance at it, it startles me as if I've not seen it before.

Her papers are scattered across the top of the desk. The title on the top page is difficult to read. There is not enough light as there's only one window and it faces the backyard.

I put her papers in the top drawer of the desk. I have some word problems to work on. Leaning toward the venetian blinds, I pull the cord to open them. Through the slats the strong autumn light enters the room. From where I stand I can see the entire backyard—my mother's sitting under the maple tree and the leaves on the ground surrounding her are a deep red color. Her crossed ankles are hidden beneath her dark green billowy skirt; the buttons on her burgundy blouse are undone. A strong breeze blows, opening her shirt, fully revealing her small breasts. I stick my fist inside my mouth, preventing myself from crying out. She's not alone. Close to her stands Mr. Martaine holding a large pad of paper in one hand, a low-burning cigarette between two fingers. His other hand moves quickly across the sheet. He sketches freely, unmoved, it seems, by the sight of her breasts. Yet, when his head's down and he's concentrating on his sketching, his expression is earnest. I snap the blinds shut, yanking the window cord with my free hand. I keep my fist in my mouth and run upstairs and into my bedroom, lock the door, get into bed, under the covers. As I lay there I replay in my mind my mother's calm, steady expression, her small breasts, Mr. Martaine's impartial, sweeping glance, the quick movement of his hand as he sketched. And I wish the maple tree was not so close, so easy to view from where I stood. It was as if I was looking between the slats through binoculars, and my mother and Mr. Martaine were unnaturally close to me, every detail of their beings exposed, enlarged by the strong lens. Though my mind is racing, my heart thumping beyond my control, I remain quiet and still beneath the covers, as if any movement on my part will draw attention to my whereabouts.

I hear them open the back door and come into the kitchen, their voices low, weary. I block my ears, not wanting to know what they're saying to each other. I lay in bed with my eyes tightly closed and imagine my mother insisting that he stay, her expression pleading, her hair falling down past her shoulders, her blouse opening. I press my hands even more firmly against my ears and hold still in this position, yearning to roll in the leaves.

The year my mother knows Alex Martaine she becomes more and more beautiful. She sheds her self-consciousness as if it's a shawl she's let drop to the floor. She wears her usual style of clothing and her hair is the same as always, long, slightly unfashionable. Her tone of voice is still high-pitched and edgy at one moment, subdued and compliant the next. The change in her is quite subtle. No longer does she move about swiftly and a little unevenly. Instead, she steps forward more slowly, more confidently, her eyes watchful.

I often find her walking about the house in a loose, thin

robe, her breasts partially exposed, seeming fuller than when I saw her out in the backyard posing for Mr. Martaine.

The year goes by in a flash. I compare it to how it is when you observe a painting. When you connect with a work of art for a moment or two, you experience a sense of timelessness, a poignancy that is swiftly gone once you step back into everyday life. For us, during this year, not one hour is like everyday life.

Over Christmas dinner my father sits sideways in his chair, his legs crossed and tells us between gulps of red wine that he's about to make a breakthrough in the novel he's working on. "What is it about?" my mother asks in a distracted voice, caressing her glass with the palm of her hand.

"A surprise," he answers, raising his eyebrows, blushing.

"Teasing?" she asks in a voice devoid of expression.

My throat tightens; I long to get up from the table but force myself to stay, to watch.

~

He leaves the next day. I stand near the front door, my mother behind me, waving good-bye to him. He drives off into the winter dusk, his car lights bright beneath the darkening sky. She doesn't wave but nods her head, her complexion pale, her fine crescent-shaped brows raised as if she's frightened. I feel the pressure of her hand resting on my shoulder. I lean back and rest my head against her chest, feel the rapid beating of her heart.

Silent, she closes the front door, then walks toward the study at the end of the hallway. I follow her and find her standing at the window facing the backyard, staring outside at the icy cold ground and the bare maple tree. I shiver, recalling the breezy day I saw her under the tree posing for Mr. Martaine, yellow and red fallen leaves covering the ground.

The trolley is crowded and drafty. My mother and I huddle together in a shared seat. We both raise our eyes to a tall man with a briefcase standing before us, his knees bumping ours every time the car lurches sideways. She doesn't speak; she wears a steady, concentrated look, her eyes a bit moist as if she's tired, as if she's forcing herself to make this trip. Her gloved hand grips my shoulder for support; I feel her sense of anticipation through the thick material of my hooded coat.

When we arrive at the museum, there's only one guard in the entranceway and no other visitors in sight. Our footsteps echo as we slowly ascend the marble steps to the second floor. My mother walks with her chin raised, melting snowflakes spotting her exposed hair and face. She's slightly out of breath from the climb, and though she's grasping my hand tightly, she appears calm, her eyes gleaming.

When we reach the threshold of the room, she lets go of my hand and walks alone across the shiny parquet floor. I stand in the wide doorway next to the guard, who's sitting on a plastic folding chair. She stands in the center of the room, her hands slightly held out away from her body, as if she's a ballerina about to assume a pose. Then she walks in her new slow and assured way toward a large painting that nearly covers the expanse of one wall and stands before it. Gauguin's masterpiece. She's confident and exhilarated in a quiet way, her lips moving slightly.

I quietly stand next to her, careful not to touch her, not to intrude on her thoughts. The expression in her eyes softens and her lips form a light smile. The painting pleases her; it means more to her, I believe, than the exotic colors and gentle naked people. She's had a print of this work hanging on the wall in the study for as long as I can remember.

There's no one else in the room other than the two of us and the guard, who now paces back and forth in front of the plastic chair. The high ceiling is intimidating; in this room I feel lost. As I turn to gaze at a Renoir, I hear strong, pronounced footsteps. When I look over, I see Alex Martaine standing next to her. His appearance is sudden—it's as if he's shown up abruptly and irrelevantly in the middle of one of my dreams.

Mr. Martaine's coat, black-and-white tweed, has little dots of white wool sprinkled all over it like wedding rice. At first I do not hear what he's saying, just the tone of his voice. He sways slightly forward when he speaks, the sound of his words all consuming.

He puts one hand on her shoulder and with his other one he points to the painting. My heart begins to race. While my mother looks at the Gauguin, I am hot and uncomfortable.

"The shadows are what interest me," he says, "how Gauguin uses them to influence color." His voice now is mellow, lilting. Fleetingly, I am entranced. "And this subject here," he continues, lowering his finger, "androgynous—isn't he? She?" My mother remains quiet. I turn to look at her—I want to know which figure he is speaking of. But she's no longer studying the Gauguin. The spell of the painting's been broken. She gazes at Mr. Martaine, now more interested in him, in his presence. Her eyes unwavering, she steps closer to the painter.

I go over to the brown leather seat in the middle of the room. I'm feeling sick. Soon I hear her call out my name. When I look up, she beckons me to follow her. Her eyes are wide open, her mouth fixed. Mr. Martaine stands behind her, intently watching my mother as if they are alone. He slides his hands in and out of his coat pockets, appearing uneasy.

~

The wind is sharp and cutting as we cross Huntington Avenue. Newly fallen snow blankets the sidewalk. We find a small coffee shop and we're soon seated by the lone waitress, an elderly woman in a heavy black sweater and a matching woolen headband.

My mother sits across from me, next to Alex. Now I'm shivering. "She's always cold," she says in a pleased voice, nodding at me.

He stares at me in a concentrated way as if I've misbehaved. My throat feels prickly, tears come to my eyes. "Pity she doesn't live in a warm climate," he answers curtly. Then he looks away and focuses his attention on my mother. And I think of the Gauguin painting, the half-naked people, the rich colors, and I am warm and dizzy.

Alex Martaine speaks only to her. I believe his words have more than one meaning to them—it's as if he's speaking a foreign language, one that my mother completely understands and is as equally fluent in as he. He opens his coat a bit. His fingers are long and restless; he picks up a small salt shaker and plays with it.

"You have a good appreciation of Gauguin," he says, throwing her a sidelong look.

She nods, turning her head away.

"He's compelling," she answers, smiling at me.

"Some people feel uneasy, voyeuristic. They step back and think, 'No, I am not going there.' I've never quite understood this—it is only a painting," he says.

"Ironic—aren't you," she says hastily and smiles.

Then he shoots a glance at me before turning to her. "Oh, Lil, I've decided to go to Paris next summer to work. Will you come?"

She looks directly at him and says willfully, "I don't know, Alex. You're asking too much." Instead of squinting as she does when she's upset with my father, her eyes are open, steady.

"Is it really too much, Lil? You have a rather liberal husband."

"You can be cruel," she says firmly, her fist brushing the table.

"He's the one in New York. You know I like him."

"Alex, please." There's a hard edge in her voice now—I've never before heard her anger. It frightens me.

"Must be going now," he answers evenly, tapping the table with his long, agile fingers. He stands up, leaving his cup of coffee untouched. There's no trace of emotion in his voice, no change of expression in his round brown eyes and long face.

She doesn't watch as he walks out the door; she just looks down at her cup for the longest time, as if it's a piece of modern sculpture she's studying because she finds it puzzling.

As we walk out of the coffee shop, she tells me, now sounding impatient, that she will hail a taxi. I'm relieved as I am weak and do not have the energy to walk to the trolley.

~

We leave the city, huddled together in the back seat. As the taxi slowly moves across the wide, steel bridge not far from our home, the snow, which stopped for a while, begins to fall thickly again. The driver stares out at the road before him.

My mother gently puts her arm around me and with her other hand she touches my face, then my forehead.

"You are burning up, dear—you must be sick. I've neglected you," she says, her voice both strange and tender, her eyes shining triumphantly.

When he opens the door, I feel a shock of cold air wafting into our home, up the stairway and into my room. Just as on a warm early autumn day we may think for a moment it's July or August, on this cold early March morning it is as if we're still in the midst of winter instead of moving toward spring. I hear a thud on the tiled floor of the foyer as he drops his heavy suitcase.

At my bedroom window, I look out at the falling snow clinging to the bare maple tree in our backyard, thinking how barren everything appears despite the fresh white blanket spreading across the yard.

"I'm back," he calls out. His tone is flat and puzzled as if he's uncertain about where he is and wondering if he possibly may have entered the wrong home.

He has never returned from New York before without letting us know first.

I hear my mother's hurried footsteps, imagine her motion fanning the chill in the air. There's silence. I believe she's hugging him, then quickly drawing away, her expression both earnest and distant, her lips pressed together.

"What do you mean you're back? You are always back, and then you are away again," she says, a trace of suspicion in her voice.

"I'm not returning to New York," he answers so feebly that although I am standing above them at the top of the stairway, I nearly miss his words. "I've given it up."

"What happened?" she asks, her tone now surprised—there's a roundness to it, a depth I've never before heard.

"I am unable to write a word. I realized I just wanted to get away, to escape. I only thought I wanted to become a novelist; I didn't actually want to write. I've discovered I am not suited to it—I am not who I thought I was."

"Don't be foolish. No one is who he thinks he is. We all have many sides, often conflicting; we are misguided if we think otherwise," she says, her voice sounding sharp and confident.

As I walk slowly down the stairway, I am bolstered by the authority in her voice.

He studies me as I come toward him. "I'm home," he says softly, his eyes weary, a bit swollen, his lashes thick. "Happy to see me, Jocelyn?" He is distant, out of sorts.

"Yes," I say forcefully. Yet I'm more anxious.

He bends over and hugs me weakly. Then he turns to my mother, his eyes pleading; he presses her hand inside both of his. Leaving his suitcase in the foyer, he continues to grip her hand, and as if he's ushering her into a dark cave, he leads her up the stairway and into their bedroom. Quietly and firmly he shuts the door.

For the remainder of the winter through early summer, I watch my parents at a distance, not needing to get too close, and yet at the same time not wanting to be too far from them. I believe if I'm away for too long something untoward will happen.

Every day I hurry home to them, and whenever I'm even slightly under the weather, I'll tell my mother I'm not feeling well enough to go to school. Yet there's no tension between my parents to cause me to behave in such a way. They're more relaxed than they've been in a long time. They speak to each other in quiet voices as if awed by their new togetherness.

Over dinner my mother toys with her food, then abruptly puts down her fork and with one thumb twirls her wedding band around her finger. She smiles slightly, her eyes drifting, her face thin and worn. My father eats in a steady, concentrated way, never speaking very much. Easily and thoughtfully he answers any question that either my mother or I ask him.

I become more silent and taciturn in their presence. Often, I eat quickly, excuse myself, and say I have homework to do. I find a spot in the house where they'll not be able to easily see me—in the alcove beneath the staircase, or behind the French doors in the living room—and I watch them with notebook in hand, pretending to study.

In my hiding position, I sketch my parents' faces and bodies with a sharp pencil. My lines are not straight, my figures look wavy. Yet I try to capture the emotion on their faces in order to better understand them.

My newfound detachment gives me a sense of power. I try to show the confusion on my father's face by drawing him with an open mouth and wispy brows. My mother is more difficult to sketch. Her eyes are always wandering and alert, yet she doesn't seem to smile very much—though she never looks sad either. One cold spring day I'm nearly in tears as I attempt to draw her. In the living room she is stretched out on the sofa next to the fireplace; an open book is splayed facedown across her chest. As she languidly raises her arms, she encircles one wrist with her other hand, the light from the flames playing across her expressionless face. I don't know how to begin my sketch. I press my hand over my mouth so she will not hear my sobs.

Que Sommes-Nous
What Are We?

1973–1974

Each day in class Mr. Martaine wears a thin, short-sleeved white shirt, even when it's cold and snowy outdoors. Just as the clock on the firehouse strikes noon, he pushes open a window in the far corner of the room, his tie flipping from a gust of wind. Then he sits on the sill and intently smokes a cigarette, looking off into the distance at the clouds or at a plane flying overhead. He smiles loosely, revealing a sense of contentment that eludes him when he's teaching.

At seventeen I know he's not simply Mr. Martaine, but Alex Martaine, a Canadian painter, well respected in some circles in Boston and New York, not yet widely known. It's said he's teaching at Pierson Academy because it's close to Boston, a short drive over a heavy steel bridge, and he needs to make ends meet.

Class begins at eleven thirty and is held on the third floor, at the back of the high school auditorium in a roped-off area next to a baby grand piano. The hardwood floor is highly polished, the smell of wax strong and unrelenting.

Whenever it's rainy and dark, I'm comforted to know that in a classroom on the floor directly below us, my father, in his thoughtful way, is teaching literature, his cheeks slightly flushed.

On this day the auditorium is filled with sunlight shining through six long windows. With a piece of charcoal in my hand, I stand before my easel, my heart beating steadily as I wait for Mr. Martaine.

On the threshold, he casts a solemn glance across the room and then enters. Tall and slouching, he makes his way through the class, stopping before each easel to comment. His deep-set eyes are round and brown, his cheekbones high and flat, and his sleek hair falls unevenly to the left. His lips are full and his chin juts forward, creating the impression he's either angry or tentative, or perhaps both.

It's his wry expression I find most intriguing; it's as if he's forever reminiscing about something disconcerting and painful.

I wonder if he's pondering his marriage, which took place a year after he arrived in the city of Pierson, before he knew my mother. The marriage lasted about ten months. It's rumored that his wife, a dark-haired, vivacious woman, found him moody and intolerable. His dedication to his work depressed her. They lived together in a house across from the ocean. And as Pierson Academy is close to both the ocean and Mr. Martaine's dwelling, the handful of us who are intrigued by him often pass by after school, hoping to see the ghost of his ex-wife. Or we'll attempt to peek into a window to catch sight of the easel she smashed before she left him. It's rumored he found it in an antique store in Paris and, unbeknownst to the owner, it once belonged to a famous painter.

I readily believe the story about Mr. Martaine's ex-wife, how in a jealous rage she smashed his favorite easel. His solitude and his single-mindedness allow me to feel slightly superior, yet at the same time, because of his talent and because he knew my mother, I am at a distance from him.

At the beginning of class, when he first walks into the room, I think of him with my mother in front of the picture window, how close together their bodies were pressed. My heart no longer steady, my throat dry, I then recall my mother's friend Gracie, who moved away from Pierson around the time of the affair.

But once class begins I focus on steadying my easel, choosing colors, working with light and shadow, and holding my brush or charcoal correctly. Mr. Martaine becomes like any other teacher, the recent past seeming very far away.

On the side wall of the auditorium, above the piano, Mr. Martaine has taped a print of Gauguin's masterpiece. The edges of it are stained and frayed. He never refers to the painting in class but one rainy afternoon he drives the twelve of us in a small school bus to the museum to see the original. Although he discusses the other works he points out this day—the two Renoirs, the three Manets, and a few seventeenth-century Dutch paintings—he doesn't say a word about the Gauguin, allowing each one to experience it in her own way.

We stand crowded together before the Gauguin. As I study the painting I inwardly recoil from it. Each subject in the painting seems aloof from his or her neighbor, preoccupied and bored—a boy reaching up to pluck a piece of fruit from a branch, a woman standing alone in the background, a baby lying on a rock in shadow with a bland expression, an older child eating an apple as if it is a tedious chore. But the colors are rich and exotic, out of keeping with the detachment in the characters' faces. The more I look at it, the more I realize the vibrant colors are what cause the painting to appear so still. The uninhibited sensuality oppresses me, entraps me.

When we return to class, I peer up at the print on the wall above the piano, unable to avert my gaze from that strange and disturbing scene.

One wintry morning, snow falling thick and pearly, clouding the windowpanes, Mr. Martaine announces that, unlike many of his contemporaries, he's been most influenced by the Group of Seven painters.

He sits on top of his desk with his legs crossed and strokes his chin with his thumb and forefinger. Then he turns to look up at the Gauguin print above the piano. Not certain who the painters are, I am embarrassed by my lack of knowledge and afraid to ask as it seems so important to him. Though he is rarely short with any of his students, I do not want to chance a stern reaction and break his reflective mood. I listen raptly, hoping to discern something about the Group of Seven to help me feel more connected to my teacher.

With a trace of emotion in his voice, his eyes still, he tells us about the very blue sky in Jackson's *A Quebec Village,* the softness of winter in MacDonald's *Snowbound,* the swirling wind in Varley's *Stormy Weather.* And by the end of his vivid and encompassing lecture, I learn not as much about the Group of Seven painters as I do about how much my teacher loves his country of birth, how deeply he is inspired by Canada's landscape.

A bright and windy day in early spring, I walk with my one friend, Luanne, past Mr. Martaine's home. His car is not in the driveway. We drop our backpacks on the front lawn, then go to the side of the house and peer into a window, hoping to catch sight of the patched-up easel. Sunlight floods the room, and we instead see a painting startlingly close to us, propped up against two stacked sofa cushions. It is of a nude male, his body in profile, one of his knees raised, the other one lowered. As the head is turned away, I cannot see the face. But the form is strikingly familiar. Shaken and then numbed, I press my face hard against the windowpane, flattening my nose and mouth until I need air.

Warm May drifts through the half-open windows of the auditorium. Art class is in session. The model, a woman dressed in a beige leotard, stands on a narrow platform to the left of the piano, her features the color and texture of putty, her arms outstretched and her ankles crossed as if she's pinned to a cross. With a two-inch piece of shaved charcoal in my hand, I draw her form.

Mr. Martaine approaches my easel and lowers his head to examine my work. His gaze is sharp and sweeping, his scent a blend of cigarette smoke and oil paint. In a flat, aloof voice, he says, "Jocelyn, do not draw the model—for God's sake, it's not about how well you draw, it's about how well you see. Sketch the shadows surrounding her and her figure will emerge."

I look up at him, now reading restrained impatience in his somber eyes. Resolutely, I answer, feeling my face redden, "But you *see,* I want a more abstract interpretation; I don't want her figure to fully emerge."

He returns my stare. In a soft, steady voice, he says, "You will." And as he walks away, his leg brushes mine.

Summer. A haze of light encircles the kitchen the morning I tell my parents I've decided not to go to Europe with them. I will be fine, I say—I am nearly eighteen. My mother is not convinced; she avoids my gaze. But when she speaks, her tone is precise, confident. I have come to realize she prefers how she is now. She works at the museum, giving tours from time to time.

My father is willing to travel to Europe without me. But she does not want to leave me behind. One hand splayed across her chest, she pleads with me to go to Florence with them, to the Uffizi, to see all the brilliant works, especially Botticelli's

La Primavera, her favorite. I will understand it better now, appreciate it more than I did when we were all there together four years ago. Her voice strong, her eyes gleaming, she lightly slaps her hand on the table and says, "God, I could stand in front of that painting for hours."

As I drive them to the airport, I feel a grand sense of freedom. Once my mother and father disappear inside the terminal, I smile, truly smile—broadly, deeply. I have not done so in so long, perhaps never before.

Luanne, tall and knowing, her eyes deep brown, comes to stay with me. On many nights we go to parties with men who are already in college and are home for the summer. We become more daring. I explore and hold my secret close.

During the mornings we work at a day camp, showing children how to make figures with clay. On the nights we stay home, we read Kazantzakis, Roth. We imagine what college will be like.

My parents return, flushed with the joy of having been abroad. My mother tells me I have changed. "What happened?" she asks, raising her crescent-shaped brows. "Nothing," I say, turning away.

Soon I leave for college.

1976

I do not learn until much later what my father knows about Mother and Alex Martaine. He reveals his emotions when I least expect him to, when I believe Mother's past affair has lost its significance in our lives.

It is a late January night. There is no snow on the ground but it has been a frigid winter; the temperature has not risen in weeks. In my dark, cool dorm room, I sit at the edge of the mattress. Facing me is Hal, his shoulders touching the back of the chair he's pulled close to the bed. His hair is brown and wavy, his palms broad, his eyes hooded, his face long and sculpted. I believe I love him.

He leans forward, gingerly holds my hands, tells me he's met someone closer to his age. He is twenty-four, a graduate student. Tears crawl down my face. He's exhilarating to be with. He's encouraged me to become more expressive in every way. "I'm sorry," he says, looking down at his shoes, his ankles turning in. "You are so intense," he says. "At first I found your intensity erotic—but you are only nineteen," he adds, looking lost.

I call home, knowing my father will be the one to answer; my mother sleeps soundly. It's easier to confide in him; his nature is much more philosophical than hers. She will blame and be swift in her assessment of what's happened. This is how her maternal instinct expresses itself.

When he picks up the phone, his voice sounds alert. He putters around the house at all hours, restless in his slow-paced way.

"I need to see you—something has happened," I say. I don't sob or reveal any distress, yet he understands. He pauses for a moment, doesn't say anything. He's silently evaluating my words, purposely devoid of emotion. But he knows me and he knows the less I say, the steadier I sound, the more devastated I am.

All he says is, "I'll be there in three hours." When he arrives, he appears dismayed, as if he's just awakened from a confusing dream.

He sits not on the chair but at the edge of my bed, his face crinkled up like a newborn's, his light red hair sparser since I last saw him. The soft, dim bulb in the dorm room keeps him mostly in shadow, giving him a sense of freedom; he can speak without fully being seen.

His approach isn't what I expect. Instead of inquiring about what I've experienced, he tells me about what happened when he went to New York. "Sometimes it's easier and more helpful to hear someone else's past trials—sometimes that helps more than rehashing an experience, still so close to you," he says, lowering his head, avoiding my tear-filled gaze.

He confides much to me that winter night, the bare trees standing outside the window, the sky bleak, dawn some hours from breaking.

What I learn is my father's experience in New York did not turn out as he expected. His first goal was to write a novel, and his second was to have an encounter with a woman he did not know—a stranger, he says. He was searching for poetry, adventure. Neither of those things happened. Sitting for hours in front of a blank sheet of paper, whether it was hanging from a typewriter or in a notebook, made him uneasy. His imagination wouldn't work. He didn't like the blankness of the page—instead of arousing his creative juices, he felt hollow inside. He prefers people, not characters. And so he realized he is a teacher after all and there's nothing wrong with that.

"What's more alive than teaching? There's an art to it as well," he says, meeting my gaze.

He met a woman in New York. He slips this out in an opaque way, so opaque that it takes a while for me to realize what he's implying. And yet when I become aware of his meaning, I also understand he desired to know about her, to form some sort of attachment. He dislikes adultery; he isn't suited to it. It isn't in his nature.

"Life isn't literature, Jocelyn. That's been my mistake all along—I've confused the two."

~

Shaking his head, he tells me that for some reason—perverse perhaps—he wanted my mother to have a relationship with Alex. When he accepted the fellowship in New York, he believed he was pursuing his dream of becoming a writer. But soon after he arrived, he realized her passion for Alex Martaine had been driving him all along.

He had much time to reflect when he was away, and for him, pondering too much while alone is not a good thing; he becomes melancholic. But this time it was helpful. Maybe, he says, because of all the activity in the streets, he could never truly feel sad in New York. He knew how much he wanted her to be with Alex, and yet he was frightened of his desire as well.

"But he was your friend too," I interject, my arms crossed as I pace before him.

"We were close," he says, lowering his head.

Then, rubbing his hands over his knees, he continues, tells me what he eventually concluded was that the relationship would not last. Their temperaments were too different.

"Lilly, your mother, is too much of a rebel; she wouldn't want to attach herself to someone as committed to his work as Alex is."

And so he believed that once he returned home, he and my mother would resume their life together.

"It wasn't easy for me to be honest with myself—it never is for anyone," he says.

I am struck by the expression of awe on his solemn face. I cry no more.

1983

From my apartment window I watch cars splash through the water-soaked city street. It is a rainy Saturday afternoon in late May. For five years I've been living close to Harvard Square.

Now, across the road, a middle-aged couple hurries to the entrance of a Chinese restaurant with a red-and-gold-painted façade. They pass a musician, strumming a guitar, dressed in a hooded rain slicker, sitting cross-legged under the restaurant awning.

During the week, I teach second grade at a nearby public school. I am not a very promising teacher—I am annoyed with a child if he has trouble reading or if he's not behaving. At those times I long to walk out of the classroom. As I make my way to the café at the end of my street, this is weighing on my mind, along with a growing awareness that I have been unable to sustain a mature relationship, that I've never really connected with anyone.

With my head down, covered by the hood of my jacket, I open the heavy glass door of the café. There are only two other customers. As I go toward the counter, I hear a vaguely familiar voice ordering a cappuccino. A man with pensive blue eyes and a wet trench coat turns toward me. I know him and continue to stare at him to be sure he is who I think he is. When he notices me, I smile hastily.

For a moment he studies me, his gaze hesitant but curious. His mouth is slightly open. I don't recall his reticence; it is something he's learned over the past years, or maybe it has always been part of him and I simply do not know him well enough to comprehend who he really is. His eyes fasten on mine and with a heavy voice he says, "We know each other."

"Yes, you are Robert," I say slowly, blushing from a memory of my youth when I went to bed with him all those years ago, half-drunk and willfully carefree, the summer before college.

"And you are Jocelyn," he says carefully. "It was about ten years ago."

My heart races—for I feel the past overtaking the present.

We move toward a small table in the far corner. Outwardly we are hesitant, polite, yet on a deeper level we are quite certain of each other.

The café, usually sunny and crowded, is nearly empty today, damp and dark. Our table is covered with a newspaper. Robert folds it and places it on a chair. Then he turns toward me, his expression intent. He's become more distinguished over the past ten years. No longer is he a precocious and impetuous twenty-one-year-old. In his early thirties now, he carries himself like a man nearing forty. It is his overall reserve I find enticing, as I've experienced some years of exposing myself to a few lovers, revealing to them the very depths of who I believed I was. From the start, Robert's caution relaxes me, as I know I will never have to disclose to him any more of myself than is necessary.

We walk toward the high-rise building next to the café where he's recently purchased a condominium. Standing apart, riding the elevator, we are familiar and at the same time dissociated from each other. Robert looks up at the lighted ceiling and, staring at him, I recall in flashes our last meeting, his enclosing naked shoulders, his earnest expression.

He shakes off the water from his umbrella before putting his key into the lock. The apartment is cluttered from his recent move, though the piles of books and boxes are neat and orderly. It is as if I've come home.

"It is coincidental, our meeting again after all this time," he says, repeating what he said to me in the café, but sounding more doubtful. He catches my gaze.

"You don't believe in coincidence, fate?" I ask, my voice sounding high-pitched. I recall the stories about his mother and her European lover, wondering if, or perhaps even assuming, he's distrustful of women because of her.

"Yes and no," he says, frowning. He takes my jacket and neatly places it over the back of a small wooden chair in the living room.

"I do," I say fervently. "I believe in destiny—or maybe I should say self-destiny."

He pours a glass of wine for me and then takes a bottle of beer for himself from the refrigerator. As we sit next to each other on the sofa in the middle of the room—he's not yet arranged his furniture—we talk about what we each are doing. He says he is a history professor, waiting to be tenured. And I tell him about my work, how unsuited I am to it.

We are silent for a while. I get up and go over to the window. It's no longer raining. The sky is gray with streaks of thin white clouds.

He comes and stands behind me. Brusquely, he asks, "Are you with someone now?"

"No," I say, turning around, meeting his gaze.

"Will you stay?" he asks.

"Of course," I say. As he kisses me, I smell the musky scents of beer and espresso on his breath. I press my hand against his neck to hold him close, feel the dampness in his hair.

❧

We marry two years later, almost to the date. Lust is a funny thing—antithetical to passion—its silence is what reverberates most, like the stillness in the air before a storm.

Où Allons-Nous
Where Are We Going?

1990

Rain strikes the windowpanes, forming rivulets, blurring my view of the bare oak and stone cottage across the road, the For Rent sign tilting over—it is as if I am trapped in a dream.

The school day has ended and I'm sitting at my desk in my second-grade classroom with nothing to look forward to but winter.

Robert and I, married five years, have recently chosen not

to have children. Initially we were pleased about this decision—naïvely so, perhaps. For our life together has lost its elasticity. I thought we were for the most part a flexible couple—was not that our strength? But we have begun to change. We've become less accepting of each other, more judgmental of others.

Robert often paces in his study, looking pale and uncertain. He's dissatisfied with anything he writes. I'm short with him, with everyone. Our life has come to a standstill. And neither of us wants to admit that it has. We remain insistent in our belief that we are going forward with our pursuits, that we're living an exciting and challenging life as a couple and as individuals. The more we delude ourselves, the more restrained we are toward each other.

On this rainy November afternoon, I look down at the lesson plan book on the desk in front of me. I prefer a book to a computer; it's something tangible, not virtual. It's something I can touch, bend, and fold over. As I write down the lessons for the coming week, I print neither too assiduously nor too carelessly, but calmly, perhaps a little distractedly.

Except for the sound of the rain, there is near silence in the classroom. The building is brick and old, always overheated. From time to time I hear a pounding coming from the radiator.

There's one student still in the classroom: Billy. He's a shy, sullen child, surprisingly small for his age, for his parents are tall. They're intellectuals, I think, or they present themselves as such. Often during class Billy rests his head on the desk as if he's too tired to do any work. I leave him alone because there's nothing false or precocious about him. Yet despite his lack of guile, he's the one child in my classroom I do not feel at ease with. There's one every year. He's quick at learning to read words, difficult ones, yet he's not interested in the content of a story or the characters like most other children are. I wonder if his parents have not spent much time reading to him.

Billy stymies me—as direct as he appears, I know he's not what he seems; there's much brewing beneath the surface. And as I feel I'm only a middling teacher, I'm frustrated, believe I'm not insightful enough to help him. A more skilled teacher would help him focus more on his work than on his sadness. I, on the other hand, am too respectful of his mood.

Last week at the Halloween party, Billy was the only student in the class who refused to wear a costume. And because of this, my eyes were on him at all times that day; I was afraid his classmates would treat him as an outcast. He sat quietly at his desk, three cupcakes neatly placed before him, while the other children roamed about with flushed faces and excited, high-pitched voices, wrapped pieces of candy spilling over the tops of their desks.

Billy plays with the Legos I've given him to occupy his time while he waits for one of his parents to come. The ticking of the old clock on the wall behind me makes me more aware of the passing time. I might be late meeting a friend.

When I look up from my lesson book, I see tears roll down Billy's face. He sits with his hands folded. The box of Legos is on the floor next to his desk, tiny pieces scattered across the linoleum. I hesitate before I go to him.

Just then I hear a sound at the door, and when I turn around I see Billy's father standing in the threshold, his hair wet from the rain.

He's in his late thirties; his expression exudes confidence. In the way he half smiles, I wonder if he's somewhat cynical. There is some character in his face, not the kind that reveals an ethical nature, but rather one that suggests experience, hard won. Is he happy or sad? Content or discontented? He's neither—that's what draws me to him. He's tall, too thin, with dark, ponderous eyes and a bemused expression. His complexion is pale as if he's recovering from a bad flu. Though he's never really caught my attention before, I've noticed him from a distance at the end of a school day, waiting for Billy next to his car. Billy's mother is the one who comes to the parent-teacher conferences. She looks me straight in the eye, asks direct questions about her son, interrupting me whenever I attempt to make an excuse for his lack of progress in certain areas, preferring to give her opinion.

From school records I know Billy's father is a freelance journalist who works mostly from home, that he's the one who's been named to pick Billy up from school every day. I believe his first name is Max. Billy's mother is a research scientist who works in a lab at a Boston hospital.

He's an intrusion in my secure, well-organized classroom. His presence is like an unexpected chilly breeze on an otherwise temperate day. "Come on, Billy," he calls, avoiding my gaze. His voice sounds curt and his words are halting. Billy promptly goes to him. Not looking at me, he abruptly walks away with Billy in tow. I hear his uneven footsteps down the hallway as if he's pausing before each complete step.

I don't see Max again until the day before the December break. He brushes back his hair as he walks into the classroom holding a bouquet of yellow roses wrapped in silver foil. When he hands them to me, there's a dull click, his gold watch hitting mine. Many parents send gifts to me before the holidays begin. Yet it's always the child who presents me with a box of candy, homemade cookies, or flowers.

In a dark blue suit and an open beige trench coat, he's less of an intrusion in my classroom on this day. He looks away and as he does I study him; he has a longish nose and there's an impatience about him.

Talking excitedly, carrying presents, the children begin to leave the room with their parents, who were invited to come and observe for the final hour of the school day. Close to Max, his son stands quietly. He instructs Billy to wait for him at the front door of the school and soon we are alone. My heart starts to beat quickly. I'm unable to move or speak.

A group of children walking down the corridor past my classroom incessantly chant, "It's snowing, it's snowing!" I look across the room, out the window, at the snowflakes falling in large white clumps onto the roof of the stone cottage. When I turn to thank him, he's gone, vanished, like a ghost. But the flowers are still on my desk. I pick them up and press the roses to my chest, the foil crackling.

Two weeks pass. It's a cold late December day. The windowpanes are laced with ice. I pace in my bedroom, confined by the weather. When the telephone rings, I call out to Robert that I'll answer it.

I am not surprised to hear Max's voice—was I not waiting for him to call? I speak in a whisper, concerned my words will disturb Robert, who is in the next room writing an abstract. He may hear something different in my tone, a hesitation in my voice. For whenever I speak with a parent of one of my student's, I am direct, sometimes abrupt.

Max apologizes for the time he was late picking up Billy from school. Over the phone he sounds businesslike. He talks for a while, his voice slow, drawling, speaking words that do not seem to connect. But it is my own thought process that is erratic; I am too anxious to listen. Then he asks if he can meet with me. And I say I will set up a parent-teacher conference. And he says, no, not for that reason.

"Why?" I ask. "What is the purpose? I am your child's teacher."

"Because you are my child's teacher, because I am lonely, because my wife and I live separate lives."

"Why?" I ask again, as if I have not heard his words, listening only to the insistence and longing in my own voice. For Max, in his subtle way, has conveyed to me that there is nothing to be uplifted about in life. There is only the present; no past, no future, and no false hope. I am drawn to him because of the black-and-white quality of his beliefs—there is no mystery, no confusion. You aren't encouraged, but neither will you be disappointed.

Eventually I agree to meet him. It is a Saturday in late February. Robert will attend a conference at a ski resort in Vermont for the weekend. Before he leaves, he looks back at me in a quizzical way and asks if everything is okay. I nod energetically, disappointed he doesn't see through me—Robert is usually perceptive in a practical, encompassing way.

In the afternoon I take the subway into Boston and meet Max at a pub. After lunch we go to his car and he drives back to Cambridge, to the stone cottage across from the school. The For Rent sign has been removed.

Inside there are three rooms: a bedroom; a small kitchen with a narrow stove and a microwave above it; and a sitting room with an oval braided rug and a rocking chair, the front legs scuffed, so still as if no one has sat in it in years.

The mid-afternoon sun, a mellow golden light, suffuses the bedroom. The spread on the bed is a soft cotton quilt, a pumpkin color. And I think of Halloween, how much I disliked the holiday when I was a child because those you knew hid behind masks and you were never certain of someone's identity—not even your own when you looked at yourself in a mirror wearing a disguise.

When I drop my pocketbook onto the floor, the sound echoes. I feel the cold and unwelcoming strap against my foot.

Max goes over to the window and closes the blinds. The light in the room is dimmer now, casting shadows over the pillows, the table beside the bed. It's as if I've been here before.

As he comes toward me, I see uncertainty in his expression. A shadow crosses his face, darkening the skin beneath his eyes. When he meets my gaze, I am less doubtful, drawn to his uncertainty.

Detached yet intensely willing, I pat down the collar of his trench coat.

My heart races, my throat is dry, my face feels frozen; I've never been more afraid of such dark sensuality, yet so intrigued by it at the same time.

"You are a hedonist!" I cry out, tears springing to my eyes.

Max removes his coat, tosses it over a chair. He takes off his watch and drops it onto the table—it's the same one that clinked against mine when he handed me the roses that day in the classroom.

His back to me, he hunches his shoulders forward, slowly undressing. Just standing there, my foot touching the pocketbook, I watch. My coat is open but I do not move, curious about his desire, his feral nature.

His body is long, loose, jarring, and I study him as if I'm holding a piece of charcoal, uncertain how to draw his form.

When he presses against me, I awkwardly stroke his taut shoulder. He takes my hand and together we go over to the bed. As I sit on the edge of the mattress, he kneels before me and with steady fingers unbuttons my blouse. Then he raises his lips to my mouth, his tongue against mine. I close my eyes, my hands shaking against his chest, willing myself to push him away.

When I return home, I shower. I stand directly beneath the head, raise my face so that the flowing stream strikes my eyelids. I scream and scream some more, an anguished piercing scream as if I've just missed being hit by an enormous truck, like the one my mother's father drove cross-country.

I take the next week off from school, tell Robert and the principal I hurt my back while lifting a file cabinet. While Robert is at work, I browse through his professional journals, knowing he has sabbatical time coming to him.

At the end of the week, sometime during the afternoon, I find what I've been looking for. There is an advertisement in one of the journals for a historian to teach one class for two semesters at a college on the Gulf Coast of Florida. Yes, I think, Robert will be able to finish his book.

When I show it to him, he is sitting at his desk in his cramped, tidy office on the second floor of our home. He looks it over carefully, then lifts his gaze to mine and says in a low, exacting voice, "It seems as if it might suit us. I need to work on my book and you need a break, don't you?" I cannot read his expression, do not know what he is thinking.

He puts down the journal on his desk and looks away from me, out the window. "Are you back, Jocelyn?" he asks in a steady, quiet voice.

"Yes," I say ardently, and I throw my arms around his neck. But he remains still.

I refuse to see Max again. A babysitter now picks Billy up from school. She seems like a thoughtful, sensitive young woman, and I wonder if Max has propositioned her as well. He will not have any qualms about doing so.

One day, after dismissing my class, I stand in front of the school, the early March wind whipping my coat, and watch the babysitter take Billy's hand. I look across the road at the stone cottage, the For Rent sign still missing. And I think of my classroom, how it is on the day of the yearly Halloween party, all the sweat and confusion.

1991

A scar, a faint white line, runs beneath the curve of Robert's chin. Whenever he turns his head in a certain way, I notice and ask him about it. Invariably, he answers in a vague, perplexed way, telling me he was about ten years old, playing with a friend, not looking where he was heading, walking chin-first into a sliding door, the glass shattering. But his explanation always sounds unreal, as if he's presenting the synopsis of a movie he's heard about but hasn't seen.

The growing tension between us is like the steady accelerating hum of the running engine of a parked getaway car. My senses are more attuned, alerted, as if I'm speeding down a dark road, anticipating the blue lights and siren of a police car.

Since late August we've been living on a barrier island in a beachfront home two hundred yards from the Gulf of Mexico. The foliage on this narrow strip of land is bountiful and exotic. Great egrets, graceful and haunting, roam freely—quite different from New England's stark November landscape.

It's close to midnight. Warm and weary from the sudden rise in temperature, I lift my T-shirt over my head. We undress before the long beveled mirror above the low bureau. The overhead light lends a yellow pallor to our doubled selves, the few strands of gray on Robert's chest, the stubble on his jaw outlining his lone, sharp feature. His wide-set eyes are the pale color of oceans on a map. His bearing remains encompassing in a subtle way, like a tall and distant illusionist on stage—you do not realize the strength of his presence until the show is nearly over.

The house we're living in has been provided for us by the president of the newly built college on this Floridian island, where Robert has been appointed as a visiting lecturer. A small, richly decorated house, it's much more luxurious than our drafty two-bedroom colonial in Cambridge.

Robert's specialty is colonial America. I've often been encouraged by his colleagues to sit in on one of his lectures. I'm told he is a passionate, vigorous speaker. This always surprises me—I picture him as a slow, methodical lecturer who by his careful choice of words allows his students to exercise their intelligence. I imagine him injecting an anecdote from time to time that piques their interest and endears him to them.

Despite my preconceptions, and because of my overriding curiosity, one day, soon after we were married, I decided to pay a surprise visit to Robert at the university in Boston. Afternoon sun illuminated the hallway as I approached his office. I walked past the rooms of his colleagues without looking in. When I heard his voice, I stood still. Instead of his usual even tone, he was speaking exuberantly about his research to either a colleague or a student. I imagined the thoroughness of his stare and, at the same time, the calmness of his bearing. I began to feel uneasy, as if I were about to observe him having dinner with a past lover. And I realized I wasn't certain if I wanted to witness this other side of Robert. So I quickly left.

~

Robert has spent most of the evening out on the veranda studying the stars, a newfound interest of his since we've come to live on this island.

We are naked and do not touch. It's confounding to think our bodies have coupled countless times. As I eye Robert's reflection and my own, it seems impossible—the idea of the two of us as one—a figment of my imagination. For Robert our separateness is nonexistent. Whenever I mention to him how apart we seem, his eyes sharpen and he tells me, his voice vaguely ironic, that I choose to believe this and he chooses not to. This is a strength of his, the ability to be tenacious in the face of ambiguity, a strength I do not share. Instead, I am strong willed. There is a difference between tenacity and will. Together we make a rather lopsided pair.

"What did you see tonight?" I ask hastily.

"Not very much—it's too cloudy," he answers just as swiftly. It's as if neither of us is about to trust what the other will say next.

"You need binoculars."

"A telescope would be better."

For a brief moment our eyes connect in the mirror. We look uncertainly at each other, wanting to know more, but on the other hand not wanting to hear the details of what's preoccupying each of us. He has his work, the book he's writing on the Jamestown settlement; I have my conscience.

Robert turns away from my reflection, looks directly at me, his lids lowering and his mouth slightly opening. He leans over, brusquely kissing me, his outstretched hand on my back as he presses me to his chest. My heart aches as we grope our way to the floor and onto the white rug. Beneath the glow of the yellow light, despite the heat and in our strident way, we make love.

~

When I wake I check the time on the digital clock next to the bed. Three o'clock in the morning. I hear the steady whirr of the ceiling fan, blinds tapping the window frame, and the distant sound of the ocean. Robert sleeps close to me, his breathing silent and steady, his bare arm encircling his pillow.

I wrap myself in a thin white robe and walk out of our room; the material is light and clinging and I'm shaky again. For all day I've been preoccupied with the letter I received from Mother; it's affecting me in a different way now, causing me to feel both more hopeful and more anxious at the same time. Yet I only understand the angst and do not know wherein lies my hope.

Out on the veranda, I hear the roaring waves. But the breeze is mild. I switch on the light and pick up her letter from the wicker table, holding the papers close.

In her letters, she's warmer, more philosophical, optimistic. She is different from what she seems when I am facing her, physically observing her, listening to the strong, precise words she uses in her attempt to shield her receptive nature as her eyes wander like petals floating in a pond.

Dear Jocelyn,

I am writing because there is some sad news I must tell you, not fit for a telephone call. Alex Martaine is dead. Gracie wrote and told me. She is quite aged now. I hadn't heard from her in years and it was quite a surprise to hear the news about Alex and receive a letter from her as well. Remember how she just left and went out to California, supposedly to help her sister with her children? But with Gracie I never knew for sure. Her letter about Alex was very matter-of-fact, but that is Gracie, no different in old age. She must be eighty. She manages on her own, with a visit now and then from one of her nieces.

Alex achieved all he wanted to in terms of his work. He always told me that it didn't matter to him if his work was highly regarded or not—what was most important was that he painted, and continued to do so. In his way he was very humble. He must have been close to seventy. I don't know what to say or feel. I haven't told your father yet. I never know what he'll say about such things. In some way he was close to Alex too—but I am not certain how or why. It was all so long ago. He seems to be growing more and more emotional as the years pass. Things bother him more. He'll feel frazzled for a bit, and then he'll regain his old self, his old ways, and take things more in stride.

Sorry to be sending you a letter with sad news, but maybe it isn't so sad. Alex did do what he set out to accomplish in his life. How many are so fortunate?

Mother

A heavy mist hovers over the gulf; cool air carries a faint smell of salt. The foaming waves diligently tumble forth. Robert and I, out on the veranda having breakfast, look up and for a moment we listen to the silvery sound of the wind chimes hanging from the side of the house. "Enchanting," he says briskly, his eyes half-closed from the edge in the air. As he loosens his tie, his expression is thoughtful. *Enchanting* is a word he does not normally use, but in this new life of ours he's experimenting and not only with the stars. He's fully dressed for work. And I am comfortable in my white robe this breezy late January day. For after five months of living on this island, I am accustomed to the subtle fluctuations in temperature.

Robert lowers his head and smiles. In a voice as clear and defined as the sound of the chimes, he tells me about the telescope he intends to buy, pointing to the area next to the wicker chair where he wants to place the instrument.

His skin, once pale, is now tanned, and these days he uses his hands to express himself more than he ever has: he opens them up, moves them forward as if to receive what's before him. When he speaks, there's a carefree fluency to him, not the halting precision of before, and now there's an aura of contentment about him. I have always thought happiness is not part of his nature; in the past there was always a sharpness to him—often too exacting in his words or manner. He's now less guarded, more accepting.

A few yards away, there is a great egret, its head bent, its beak touching the sand. "Robert, look," I say urgently, pointing at the bird. "It's beautiful—but homely too!"

Robert studies the movements of the egret for a few moments. He turns back to me, meeting my gaze. "Yes, it's contradictory," he says pointedly, the scar beneath his chin illuminated by a fleeting ray of light.

I look away from him; my heart is pounding. I pick up the pot, pour more coffee into our cups.

"Why are we here, Jocelyn?" he asks, his voice light but testy.

"Because I have lost faith!" I cry out.

"Faith in what? Faith in me—or in your life?"

Holding my gaze, he repeats the question, sounding more resigned now. He learned resignation at a young age, maybe too young.

"I don't know," I say willfully.

"I don't have class for another two hours," he responds, his brows slightly raised, his voice mildly challenging.

In our bedroom as Robert unbuttons his shirt, his face in shadow, I go to the window and pull up the venetian blinds. On the beach I see a tall, dark-haired man bending over, picking up shells, carefully examining each one, his pants rolled up to his knees. I look out at the ocean, at the waves pounding the shore. The mist has lifted some; the sky is gray, the clouds darkening—an approaching storm.

Robert calls me; his voice is now deep and resonant, like the tone you hear when you put a seashell to your ear. My heart beats swiftly—I am uncertain. I am not yet accustomed to the new Robert. The old one—the restrained Robert—afforded me more comfort and, yes, freedom.

Before I turn to go to him, I see the lone tree near the veranda swaying in a strong breeze, palm fronds dropping onto the concrete-colored sand, the dark-haired man not deterred by the gusting wind.

Early March, a cloudy, moonless night, lights from the homes along the beach unevenly illuminate the sand. But for the gentle lapping of waves against the shore, all is quiet and still. Robert and I, longing for a cool breeze, sit back to back on a large terrycloth towel. Behind us is our dimly lit veranda, and within our reach the bottle of wine we've half buried in the sand. Intently, we stare up at the sky, as if expecting the clouds to disperse at any moment and reveal the stars.

"What would you choose to see tonight, Robert, if you could see any constellation?" I ask, hearing a focused expectancy in my voice.

He doesn't answer and I turn toward him, study the whiteness of his T-shirt, the shape of his lips, the way they naturally fall, signifying neither happiness nor sadness. The outline of his arms and legs reflects his inner solidity and tenacity. In the near darkness more is realized, and for a brief moment I know who he was as a child. I imagine what the expression on his face was when he was eight years old and he was told that his mother had left him and his father for a lover and a new country. His gaze must have been open, his body constricted, as if harnessed.

Robert has told me that when he was in his twenties, he ardently and intensely threw himself into a relationship. The women he was involved with found him emotionally naïve, and because of this he was taken advantage of, often inadvertently. Intimacy was not his forte, he soon realized. The only way for him to survive was to avoid expressing his emotions directly. Caution, circumlocution worked best for him. And so, through experience, he learned how to intellectualize his emotions.

I've known this for some time; he's spoken to me about his past relationships but it's taken me a while to piece it all together, to really know this about him. On this island with its dark nights and long silences, the simplicity of our life makes clear and real things we once thought were hazy. More is revealed in a different way, unintentionally and slowly, like the unraveling of a somewhat knotty ball of yarn by two curious and assiduous kittens.

Robert pours more wine into each glass. I cannot see his expression clearly, yet I try to intuit what he's thinking: he's questioning my loyalty to him. I know this not because he's referred to it in subtle ways, as many would have done, but because he's been more dogged in his acceptance of me, more direct in his concern that I may be wandering from him, from our marriage.

"I wish I were not so restless, Robert. I will change. I want to be a better person," I say, my voice sounding high and strained.

"How will you go about doing that?" he asks, and I can

tell by the quick movement of his head that he's afraid he'll miss my answer if he does not look directly at me, if he remains too unobtrusive. It has grown darker now, more house lights are off, and so it's difficult to read the expressions in each other's eyes.

"How does one make oneself a better person? What is it to be a better person? Fidelity to one's life? One's self? One's ideal or passion?" I ask, feeling the effects of the wine.

"Yes, yes, and yes," he says, and I feel the pressure of his hand on my knee. I now comprehend how he's accepted and dealt with his life. Perhaps he's been too clumsy, despite his attempts at being even and steady. But since we've been here, he is opening up.

"I do believe there is a way. I just haven't discovered how to be more truthful, more aware. Most of the time I feel as if I am in a maze and I don't know which way to turn."

"Have you always believed this?" Robert asks in a husky voice. His hand is now off my knee. I feel his agitation.

"I've been in a maze for a long, long time—since before I knew you—a self-imposed one. For some reason I want to be like this; I relish it as much as I hate it. Perhaps it protects me from having to extend myself, from having to commit. Yesterday I was browsing through an art book on post-Impressionism I found at the bookstore in town. I came across a series of Gauguin paintings—I've never really taken to Gauguin's work, but I remember there was a print of his masterpiece taped to the wall in my high school art class. And my mother had the same print in her study; one day I noticed it was no longer there and I didn't know how long it had been gone. I've always wondered why she liked Gauguin, his Tahitian paintings. I find his work oppressive."

"What do you find oppressive about Gauguin?"

"His work is sultry, sensual—in a hopeless, staid way."

"Sensuality has a life of its own," he says gloomily.

"How much have you been tempted, Robert?" I softly ask. My heart beats rapidly.

"Are you asking me if I've been faithful to you?"

"I know you've been loyal. I suppose I mean faithfulness in spirit."

"I believe I've been faithful to you in spirit as well as in fact," Robert answers.

"You sound as if you regret it, Robert," I say, hearing a quiver in my voice.

"Do you?" he asks sharply.

I grip Robert's arm, feel the intensity of his short, quick breath, as if it's coming from me. I know he's wondering about me. Is it better to have escaped or to have accepted desire? Desire? Desperation? What is the difference?

I cling tightly to him and the more I hold on the further away he seems. "Where are you, Robert? What are you thinking?" I cry out.

He doesn't answer. His eyelids lower and his lips part as

he slips the light robe I'm wearing off my shoulders and slowly, quietly makes love to me, gently pressing me into the sand.

Afterward, our bodies separate, off the towel, I swivel toward him. His expression is startled, as if he doesn't recognize me, but it's too dark to know for certain. "It's me," I say, lightly tickling his arm. Our laughter is deep and throaty.

We've not been intimate in a while—we've kept a distance from each other.

"Why are you so interested in the stars, Robert?"

Closing his eyes, he says, "We have given the stars names and shapes, and so they reveal man's vision of life, what man has seen, what man has imagined. Maybe they are a reflection of who we are—a circumscribed vision, perhaps, like prehistoric art. I've thought of a constellation, the Painter's Easel. It's a simple constellation, fifty-six light years away, and its stars are quite faint, yet it has one fast-moving star, the second-fastest known star—bright and elegant, I imagine."

Just as he finishes speaking, a flash of lightning crosses the sky, closely followed by a thunderous roar. We hastily gather our things and make our way across the sand to our home. While Robert is in our bedroom, I stand at the sliding glass door, watching the storm.

In the mail this morning I received a note from Mother. It's short, and quite different from any other letter she has sent to me. It's both cryptic (absent are her warm musings) and intensely personal. I am surprised by its contents. It's as if she's crossed a boundary with me and I am not certain why, or exactly what line she's crossed. She has used plain white paper, and her florid script in black pen appears stronger, more emphatic than it does when she uses paper with color.

Jocelyn,

I was at a lecture at the museum today, and one of the paintings we discussed was the same work I wrote about during the month you were conceived. It is a painting by Matisse. It is a nude of a model sitting on a table. Her expression is hard and impenetrable. You can see the reflection of the artist in the mirror behind the model. It is a painting that has always bothered me. I am compelled by it and I intensely dislike it. It is very stark.

Mother

Not certain of her purpose, I am annoyed she has sent it.

I walk the beach. The air is warm and suffocating. The waves are high and greenish in color. It's as if they are spewing warmth. The sand is too hot to go without shoes, and walking on the beach in sandals is not very comforting or relaxing. I become more distracted and annoyed.

A few yards ahead of me, I see the dark-haired man who often combs the beach in search of shells. This is the closest I've been to him. He appears much older. He has a faraway look in his eyes, and I do not walk too close to him as I'm in no mood for conversation. He appears lonely, and he's very tall, taller than Robert.

Now he's stopped to collect some shells. I wave, avoiding his gaze as I pass him. My face is wet from the spray of the waves. I look down and notice a conch shell, startling pink in the bright sun. I stop for a moment and bend over to pick it up. Holding it in my hand, I consider taking the shell home; it entices me. But I choose against doing so. I put it back down in the sand and walk some more. On second thought I turn round and decide I'll bring it home. Even in this mood, I cannot resist beauty.

But now the man is picking up the shell, holding it. It's as if he's taken what's mine. As I approach, he doesn't say anything. He offers it to me, like a priest with a communion wafer. Up close he looks even older, and for some reason I cannot take it from him. I shake my head, turn around, and walk back toward the house, tears streaming down my face.

When Robert comes home, he is smiling and not at all tired from his day or from the heat. He appears cool, as if he's moving about in a temperate, not a tropical, climate.

He's bought an expensive French wine. I watch his hands, soft, steady, and confident; he opens the bottle, popping the cork. As he pours the wine into two glasses, he asks me, his voice crisp, if I've ever been happy. Am I holding something back from him? Do I need to talk? He speaks quickly, as if he isn't expecting any answers. His look is impenetrable.

I ask him if he's saying this because I look sullen.

"No," he answers nonchalantly, "it just occurred to me I've never before asked you if you've ever been happy."

"We are married, and have been for nearly seven years—don't you know?"

"I mean before. I know you aren't now, and haven't been since we met."

"Why did I marry you then?"

"Because I calm you." And for a moment he seems mildly amused by his own words.

We carry our glasses out onto the veranda and sit in the chaise longues. I look out at the ocean—the waves are subdued, the tide has gone out.

And as if Robert has already forgotten our interchange of a few minutes before, he asks me about my day, not really listening to my responses. He's preoccupied. I imagine it's about a student or his book. I do not ask; I choose not to intrude in this world of his.

All through dinner he hums intermittently. Again, I do not ask why; I know he'll tell me his news when he's ready. At times his expression is wistful, but when he looks at me his stare is direct and penetrating, his brows furrowed in a surprisingly jovial way as if he's enchanted by life in general.

After dinner he goes to study the stars as usual. And for the first time I notice an added confidence in him, the way he tilts his head before stepping out onto the veranda.

When I join him, I see that Robert isn't looking up at the stars; he's on a chaise longue, still humming in that stop-start way of his, a little off-key, but not by much. It's the only song he ever tries: a rondo by Mozart. His humming does not make you feel uneasy as humming sometimes can; rather, it's relaxing, even though the tune is haunting. When he sees me, he sits up and grasps my hand, pulling me close to him.

"Would you like to stay here forever?" he asks, and though he hasn't switched on the light I am so close to him that I see his expression is concerned, his eyes searching. I feel his breath, surprisingly light.

"What do you mean?"

"I've been asked to stay on at the college."

Alone with Robert on this island, I think, feeling conflicted.

"Will we become part of it? Will we blend in with this unfamiliar environment?" he asks in an uncharacteristically persistent tone.

I shrug. "Let's consider it," I say, not knowing what to make of this proposition. Yet in my mind I imagine the years passing. How slow our lives will become. The loneliness of it all—having to face each other directly, no more feigning, no more escape. We've escaped to the place of escape, and now there's no place else to go.

"You are smiling, Jocelyn," he says, gently stroking my arm as if it will break if he touches it in a clumsy way.

"Why am I smiling, Robert?" I ask, my voice sounding cool against the hot night. I meet his gaze.

"You are smiling because you are happy at the thought; I think you'd like to stay. Am I wrong, Jocelyn?"

"When will it happen—officially, I mean?"

"It will happen when we agree to make our place of escape our new home," he says, holding me tightly. My head pressing against his chest, my arms around his waist, I feel the rapid beating of his heart.

May 22

Dear Jocelyn,

I remember the heavy rain and musky smell inside the church the day you and Robert were married. How the dampness crept inside the vestibule. I can still hear the sound of Gilda's high-heeled shoes striking the marble floor as she paced in front of the altar, making certain all was in order, the flowers properly arranged, before the ceremony. And how we all wanted to please Robert's stepmother because ever since Robert's mother left, Gilda had taken care of things.

That day I thought of how much responsibility I'd put on your shoulders when you were growing up. But it was a different time then and now that I realize that, perhaps I feel a little less guilty. But I do not believe I will ever completely forgive myself. Yes, it was a different time then. As adults we were more fragile because of the many changes in the world. There was the war in Vietnam that no one ever spoke about, even when we read about a death in the newspaper of a young soldier whose name we recognized, but with whose family we had never had any real contact. We just remained silent. And I felt as if I were holding myself together because the world was falling apart.

Marriage for many of us was not what we had expected it to be. I know of no one during that time who experienced a sense of solace through marriage. Perhaps we were simply imitating the larger world and all the unrest that was going on at that time. Or maybe we were deluding ourselves, thinking we were different from other generations. We really weren't you know. For as you can see there has always been trouble, sadness, and tragedy in the world.

But you were so young then, I don't know what you remember. All I can say is that as adults—as married people we not only had to find ourselves, we had to recreate ourselves if we wanted our marriage to survive—and even then there were no guarantees.

In some ways those years were quite liberating, but in other ways being an adult at that time was intensely inhibiting. You were led by desire, desire that only placed you in a corner and made you, after all, less free. But we survived—and that's important, we did survive—maybe it left us a little wobbly, a little less sure of ourselves, but we did survive.

What got me through some of this time was Gracie. She seemed not to be touched by all that was going on in the outside world, and so she was able to live her life as she saw fit.

I'll never forget the day I met her at the art history course at the museum in Boston. She was wearing a red and black scarf. I remember her telling the teacher she had purchased it in Mauritius. Even the instructor didn't know the location of Mauritius. "An island in the Indian Ocean, east of Madagascar," Gracie had said offhandedly, as if this was common knowledge. Then she was annoyed not only by the teacher's ignorance, but that of the class as well, as we stared at her in amazement.

Perhaps it was her red-gold hair, or her husky voice—she seemed larger than life. We were studying Goya at the time, and I was so fascinated by Gracie that I went and spoke to her at the end of the first class. I remember how wonderful I felt when I discovered we lived in the same city.

And then several years later when she suddenly left, and moved to California, I felt unanchored . . .

Enough of the past!

Mother

Over the next few days I read her letter again and again, as if it is notification of a prize I did not apply for—my interpretation is mostly skeptical, sometimes hopeful. She'd folded it unevenly and tucked it inside a card with a sketch of the Eiffel Tower on the front.

❧

More and more I understand the past is not easy to eschew. It's ever present, following you about, taking hold of your life with its strong grip, like an octopus enclosing its prey; but it does not strangle you, it just keeps grasping you tightly, never letting you go.

For most of my childhood I knew Robert and his family from a distance. We never socialized with them. We would see them in passing, at the supermarket, the movie theater, or school.

We knew of them because of their story: Rebecca, Robert's mother, had left her doting husband and eight-year-old son to go to live in Lisbon with her lover. I was too young to remember her, and to this day I've not met her. Robert speaks to her on the telephone once a year, on her birthday. I've only seen her in one photograph. It's a worn and faded snapshot of her that Robert keeps in his wallet. It shows her and Robert at an amusement park holding hands in front of a Ferris wheel. It's so crinkled and old that I cannot make out the expressions on their faces.

I do not know if Robert keeps it in his wallet for sentimental reasons, or because he feels obliged to carry it with him as a reminder of her.

Now all these years later we are in southwest Florida, out on the veranda, reclining in our chaise longues, listening to the roar of the gulf, glancing up at the numerous stars with our naked eyes. It's the night of our seventh wedding anniversary.

Robert, reaching for my hand, tells me, out of the blue, that when you look through a telescope you view images in reverse.

And I think how, in a sense, because of all the uncertainty in our present existence, we experience life upside down, groping through each day, our feet in the air.

Jocelyn,

I drove to City Hall today, hoping to get one last look at Alex's work on display. I had the dates confused—the exhibit closed yesterday. And when I arrived his paintings had all been taken down except one, and the custodian was about to remove it from the wall. It is a painting of a young woman. She is young, and her expression reminds me of you, though physically she is quite different. She is tall and broad-shouldered. Her hair is cut short, her cheekbones are wide, and she is standing near the ocean, wearing a sleeveless shift. You are small and narrow and you have always worn your hair to your shoulders as far back as I can remember. Yet there is a similarity between you and the figure in Alex's painting—defiant eyes and a small yet compliant mouth. It is difficult to get a true sense of her expression, as her face is covered by a shadow from the setting sun. I am not certain when he painted it . . .

As I watched him take down the painting, I realized for the first time since it began all those years ago that my relationship with Alex truly belongs to the past. Even when I heard of his death, I believed our experience somehow was still viable. But now I know it is something I will never again think about in the same way. Funny—such a simple thing as watching a painting being removed from a wall—the coldness of it, how practical and competent the custodian was as he lifted it from its spot. I felt as if a door was being shut in my face. And then I realized that I never really knew Alex. Maybe he simply suited my imagination at the time, helped me deal with my reality. For he was an artist, and I will never be able to comprehend what it is to be an artist, yet I do not know if I wanted to then, or even now. I think I preferred, and still do, the mystery of it all.

As I read Mother's words, Robert walks out of our bedroom. It's an early June morning. The sun streams in as I stand before the open sliding doors that lead to the veranda. I look up from her letter and out at the sparkling gulf. The tide has come in.

"It's official now: I am staying on at the college. I just signed the papers," he says, sounding both resigned and content.

"We made this decision a few months ago; that is when it became official for me. It is for the best," I say exactingly. But my hand trembles as I place the letter down on the coffee table.

"Are you certain you can live here?" he asks pointedly, a bit anxiously, as he's been doing repeatedly for the past month or so.

And I answer as I always do, though my tone is different today. "I think I can. There's something quite soothing about living in a warm climate year-round," I say distractedly.

"Is this out of love for me or is it because of the weather?" He asks directly, standing behind me, placing his firm hands uncertainly on my shoulders.

"You don't believe I love you?" I ask, turning to him.

His expression is vulnerable, his face drawn, his words tentative. "I want to believe you do, but I am a skeptic; I believe love in its purest form is unattainable. I've accepted this," he says with a sigh. "Life is too complicated; people's emotions are fragile, so very fragile, so filled with longing—for what, I am not certain."

"Then it is impossible for you to love me—if this is what you believe," I say, my voice high, persistent.

"You always tell me how separate we are—isn't that the same as admitting that complete love isn't really possible?" he asks.

"So that's why we are so distant from each other. Both of us at heart are skeptics."

"We have a different way of loving than most, I believe. I desire you. I've been faithful to you. Isn't that love? But that's as close as anyone can come. I think we are closer than most, or maybe as close as is possible."

I run my finger shakily across the scar beneath his chin. He looks away and I say quietly, "You used to cut yourself, Robert—I know—it has come slowly to me. I can imagine what happened. You were lonely, lost. You felt you'd been deserted. You were depressed, deeply, deeply depressed and you didn't know where to turn; you may have been fifteen or sixteen when it started. One day you were walking down the street, maybe on your way home from school. Perhaps you saw a broken beer bottle on the sidewalk and picked it up. You went home—no one was there. Then you went up to the bathroom, stood in front of the mirror, and began to nick at this spot, just beneath your chin. I suppose it became a ritual for you—maybe for a year or two?"

"It was very long ago, Jocelyn," he says, his eyes moist, his lips tightly pressed.

We hold one another closely and it seems a very long time before our gazes meet. When they do, Robert is clear-eyed, his voice determined. "And what is it, Jocelyn? I've always believed there is something about you that is hidden from me."

My heart pounds. Blood rushes to my face. I look away, out at the ocean, fearful not of the truth but of what is not true. On the beach I see the dark-haired man methodically collecting shells, his pants rolled up to his knees, a great egret close by.

I turn to Robert, press my forehead to his chest. With deep resignation I tell what I have denied for so long, about what happened the summer he and I met for the first time.

1974

A Friday afternoon, late July, Pierson Beach: I sit on a low concrete wall facing the ocean, the palms of my hands pressing intensely against the gravelly surface. The air is heavy and warm, the sky an imposing gray: a storm is about to erupt. I glance across the narrow stretch of sand and out at the sea; haze mists the line where the ocean and sky meet, humidity dampening the sharp smell of salt. The ocean waters roil in a frenzy, waves vigorously flipping, foaming, hissing. Intermittently I hear the sound of automobiles driving down the road bordering the wall.

I've been coming here every day since the school year ended. Mr. Martaine lives across the road in a small yellow house trimmed in blue. I heard he was leaving Massachusetts, returning to Canada.

I'm possessed with an overwhelming curiosity that's unpleasant. It causes me to feel uneasy and distraught; it will not go away, I believe, until I see him.

Because of the coming storm there are only a few people on the beach. I lay on the wall and feel the hard concrete against my back; closing my eyes, I listen to the waves pounding the shore. My heart beats rapidly; my desire to see him outweighs my nervousness. I intend to knock on his door, tell him I've left my portfolio from class with him, that I'll need it for college next fall.

After some time passes I open my eyes, sit up, and look down by the water. He's about fifty feet away, pacing at the water's edge, smoking a cigarette. His pants are rolled up to his knees and the waves are breaking and frothing on the sand at his feet.

My nerves are so taut I can hardly breathe. He tosses his cigarette into the ocean and turns around. His head is lowered as he makes his way across the sand toward the road. There's contentment in his stride and yet at the same time it's as if he's carrying the weight of the world on his shoulders.

He doesn't notice me. I stand up on the wall, watch him cross the street, unlock the door, and disappear inside his home.

The sky's as still as before but darker, more ominous. I jump off the wall and walk. Within moments I'm at his front door, grasping the brass knocker, banging twice. He soon undoes the latch. He stands on the threshold, his eyes bleary as if he hasn't slept in days, his trousers still wet from the sea, his bare feet sprinkled with sand.

"I've come for my portfolio," I say, my heart pounding.

"Your what?" he asks hoarsely, looking away from me.

"My portfolio from class," I answer steadily. I've never before been purposefully dishonest, yet the lie has been easy.

I am like a puppet; I don't have to do anything. I've become another person, observing my own performance. "I hear you are leaving Pierson, moving home to Canada," I say calmly. My heart's no longer racing. It's as if I've reached a different level of being, as if I'm floating. "So I have come to get it." The rain pelts my back.

"You're soaking wet, for God's sake—come in," he says bluntly.

I follow him into a room to the left of the foyer. He tells me to wait. Burgundy drapes cover the two long, narrow windows, a dark green oriental rug stretches over the hardwood floor. Despite the rain it's hot and sultry. A full-length oval mirror across the room faces the doorway. I walk over to it, study my reflection. I'm nervous and exultant, not completely the half-fearful girl-woman in the mirror with wet hair and a clinging halter dress. I see a broken easel in the corner tilting forward and I recall the rumor that it once belonged to a famous artist.

He's now standing in the doorway, staring intently at me. Our gazes meet in the mirror, his dark and forbidding, mine determined and frightened. My heart pounds wildly, my mind is numb, my knees are weakening. I turn toward him and take his hand, helping him untie the knot at the neck of my dress. As the dress falls to the floor, I feel as free and uninhibited as the women in Gauguin's Tahitian paintings; fleetingly I recall the print hanging on the wall above the piano in art class.

I turn away. Soon he's behind me; in the mirror I'm a naked, uncertain woman. I rest the back of my head against his chest hoping I'll not faint; I hear the rapid beating of his heart. He grasps my breasts as if they're made of clay.

"Have you had any experience?" His voice is frank and unaffected.

"Yes," I say, gasping for breath.

"You are lying," he answers in a curt voice, surprising me, causing my desire to subside. "As you have lied about your portfolio."

In the mirror, I see a fearful look in his eyes, but soon it's gone. I reach down and pick up my dress, wrapping it around myself as if it's a towel. I walk to the far corner of the room, still clutching my dress, holding it in place, and sit down on the sofa.

With tears rolling down my cheeks, I lower my head, focusing on the design of the rug. He walks over to me, placing his finger beneath my chin, lifting it so that our eyes meet again.

"I am going home to Ottawa," he says.

"Is it because you hate Pierson?"

He turns away.

"Did you love my mother?" I ask, my voice trembling.

"Love . . . I never finished the painting I began of her—I never could quite capture her; there was something restive about her, something unending. Love . . . I don't know. I don't know what love is. She refused to leave your father," he says candidly. "That is what I remember. She enjoyed her role as the recalcitrant woman who, in the end and all along, had just wanted to go home. There are those like your mother who rebel for the sake of rebellion, who are enthralled by it, and there are others who rebel simply to survive."

The rain forcefully strikes the windowpanes. He tosses my dress onto the floor. I shiver—not from a chill, but from the brisk touch of his hand against my breast.

"You need clothes," he says in a voice heavy with desire, giving me a chance to escape this moment, his eyes dark and unreadable.

I shake my head, decline his offer of release, for in some vague way I've known for a long time this moment would occur. I'm unable to walk away. I speak and act in ways foreign to me. I'm naked, facing a person who's also naked except for the luster of knowledge in his eyes that I'll never be able to penetrate because I'm young and without experience.

~

We do not speak much to each other; that's not the purpose of our coming together. Instead, we each fill a need in the other—a basic need, primitive, something deep and dark. And because of this we never discuss when our next meeting will be; it has to do with how much shame we feel. This sense of shame we share does not stop us. We never speak of it, though it penetrates me completely and I believe it's the same for him, as he never looks directly at me—he does everything he can to avoid my gaze. He doesn't want me to know who he is. The few conversations we have are short and sharp, and the effect is like being hit by a brisk wind on a winter day.

I go to him nearly every day in the heat of the afternoon, a time when in most homes blinds are drawn to block the penetrating rays. Even sunbathers on the beach pause at that time of day; overcome by the warmth, they sprawl out in their chaise longues or on their towels, barely lifting their heads. Only the children are active, playing in the sand, building castles with moats. On the beach I see the lethargy, the enervating effect of the sun.

I stand before his front door, bracing myself. Slowly, I lift my hand and grasp the brass knocker; it's smooth and I'm reassured. My knock is neither tentative nor forceful, but steady.

He opens the door only moments after I've knocked; it is as if he's been waiting for me on the other side. His expression is direct and at the same time noncommittal. His gaze is distant; his pupils, blending in with the dark brown color of his eyes, are nearly indistinguishable. There's the beginning of a five o'clock shadow on his lean face. He doesn't touch me; he leads me to his bedroom.

We stand in the doorway and he puts his hand on my shoulder, squinting, as if he's trying to remember something. I glance at his hand resting on my shoulder, thinking it looks much smaller and smoother than I expected.

We stare at the bed; it is not large but lumpy, the cover a burnt gold color. I feel a growing sense of dissociation. It is the only way I know how to go forward, to think and believe I'm not really there.

I watch him walk over to the bed. I don't follow him. I'm bracing myself, distancing myself even more from the moment. As he unbuttons his shirt he gazes at the painting on the wall, an abstract work in black and white—not one of his.

And then something happens. I forget myself, where I am, I don't care about anything. I am unconscious but awake. I go over to him, help him undress, and swiftly and precisely, focusing on what is before me, I remove all my clothing. I am frenetic and curious; he is composed and sensual.

It takes a few weeks before it becomes a natural act for me. I am assiduous, steeling myself each time, wanting and not wanting to be with him. He never says my mother's name and rarely ever says mine.

One afternoon he attempts to paint my portrait. I am standing close to the shore, but suddenly he stops. He says it is impossible, my expression is frozen. He isn't angry; he speaks quietly. It is as if it is his fault.

The last day I see him, the day before he returns to Ottawa, I realize I never asked him if the rumor is true about the broken easel—the one tilting forward in the sitting room—that it once belonged to a famous painter. And if so, which artist? Could it possibly be Gauguin?

I parted from him moments ago. I walk on the beach; the sun is about to set, casting a deep golden hue over the waters, the waves crashing against the shore. Tears rush down my face.

I want to turn around and walk back to him, but I don't. Something holds me back. It is because I no longer want to know if the rumor is true. I no longer adore him. I feel lost, yet I found the answer I was looking for when I first went to him.

No matter how much I tried to please him, it is my mother he prefers and maybe even loves—not me, never me.

And yet I went to the painter because I was angry with her, her desire for him—how much it influenced my life. I was looking for revenge.

But in this my mother is the winner, not me. For I know she'll never lose her passion, while mine was destroyed some time ago.

Water caresses my bare feet. I stand defiantly at the shore, knowing I am broken, believing I am free.

When Robert and I make love this night, we leave on the dim light. We are half-dressed—I in my silk slip and Robert in his light robe—not because we are impatient, but because we are tired, weary from our thoughts, our talk. Now we only need physical contact: the touch of one leg wrapped around another. The sensation of skin and material is more intimate. We avert our eyes, and then they meet. We hear the distant sound of crashing waves. We move toward each other, then away. The sighs of pleasure are richer, more consonant. Our former stridency has dissipated like loose seeds on a day with a balmy wind.

Is it the longer you are together, the more self-conscious you become, and so you are modest? Or is it the closer you are to each other, the less you need to reveal because it is already impressed in memory? I believe it has nothing to do with self-consciousness; it has to do with knowledge.

Our first year in Florida has passed swiftly. Life on this island for the most part is a drifting affair, nearly unreal. But this is not unfamiliar to me, as I now realize I have lived much of my life straddling the line between what is true and what is not. What keeps us grounded is that Robert and I have to face each other every day and see what we have become. There is no other place to run.

I've begun to draw again. I have no serious aspirations. I simply need to express myself, and this is the only way I know how.

I work only with charcoal. And I have discovered a small museum in Miami. It is about thirty miles south from where my grandparents once owned a house, where we'd visit them each summer when I was young.

Once or twice a month I drive across the state, sometimes with Robert, sometimes alone, to look at the paintings. There are special exhibitions from time to time, and I generally like the modern works more than the traditional ones. I have started to copy some of the paintings using charcoal. There is a Picasso I am fond of. And when I sketch it, I think of Mr. Martaine's art class, how he taught us to sketch the shadows surrounding a face, figure, or object. I relish the feel of the stick of charcoal in my hand, its soft, grainy texture.

~

In early December, my parents visit.

On the beach, the strong sun behind him, Father meets my gaze as I sketch his likeness. Higher than on most days, the waves crash against the shore, faintly spraying us. He is sitting on a large rock and appears more relaxed than I've seen him in a while—he doesn't seem as overtly emotional as Mother has described him in some of her letters. His legs are slightly open, his hands clasped in the space between them, his shoulders lowered. I tell him he almost resembles Rodin's The Thinker, but his posture is not quite right. He furrows his brows, smiles lazily, and then, in imitation of the statue, he puts one hand beneath his chin.

Later, he says he thinks I may have found my niche. In retirement he's taken up photography. He shows me the photographs he's taken: there is one of Pierson Academy; another is a close-up of an unusual shell; one shows a seagull riding a wave, his wings expanded; and then there is one of Mother sitting on the floor in front of the fireplace with her knees to the side, her ankles almost crossed. He's never seemed more animated. But beneath it all, and though it is not as strong as before, I sense his wistfulness.

~

As she carries my sketch book out onto the veranda, Mother says she is pleased I am working with charcoal. On the chaise longue, her eyes squinting, she studies my drawings, touching one forefinger to her cheek. Her hair is cut short and her arms are a bit fleshier, but not by much. And she does not seem as distracted as before, nor is she completely centered or grounded—she only appears more so. For a while she lingers over my sketches, but once she's finished, she gets up and hastily hands the book back to me. Her eyes half closing, she says, "I always thought your work showed promise." Then she speaks of Alex, how brilliant an artist he was and how wonderful it was that we'd known him—"He enhanced our lives, don't you think?" Not waiting for my response, she goes to the edge of the veranda, close to the palm tree, and looks out at the ocean, her chin raised, her form wrapped in the now dappling light.

Every family, I believe, possesses a prevailing philosophy. Its roots may be material, spiritual, or practical. And each member is either in accord with whatever this ideology happens to be or goes to great lengths to rebel against it. For my family, it was art, and in their eyes, the emanation of it was Alex Martaine, who brought so much to our lives, yet took from them at the same time.

From time to time and with dispassion I'll recall the summer I went to his home nearly every afternoon—or I'll think of that brisk spring day when I looked into his window and saw the painting of a nude man, the body in profile, the head turned away, the haunting familiarity of it. Then I'll remember my mother and him, their cries, their bodies pressed together, kissing in front of the picture window that balmy July night nearly twenty-five years ago, when the world was such a different place. It is an image I will always retain—it is not a painting but life, a memory that has become a part of who I am.

One morning I decide it's time to try working with oils. At the store, purchasing the supplies I will need, I recall Alex Martaine's words—*It's not about how well you draw but about how well you see,* his lecture on the Group of Seven painters, and the frayed print of Gauguin's masterpiece taped to the wall above the piano in art class. Then I think of how I will experiment with color.

~

The sight of the ocean is enticing. First I bring tubes of paint and brushes out to the veranda and set them up on the wicker table. Then I carry the easel onto the veranda and put it down not far from Robert's gleaming white telescope. I see that it is not steady. I purchased it hastily at a flea market a few months ago and then stored it in a back closet at home. I was drawn to it because it has the same black lacquer finish as the Chinese screen in Gracie's old apartment.

Either the wooden floor of the veranda is uneven or one of the easel legs is slightly off balance. But I am not deterred. The foaming gulf is before me. Standing before the easel, I cradle it with one hand until it is steady. And with my free hand, I paint.

www.ingramcontent.com/pod-product-compliance
Lightning Source LLC
LaVergne TN
LVHW090959080826
845145LV00003B/1063
9780999400678